CYCLING CHAMPION

BY JAKE MADDOX

Text by
MARTIN POWELL

Illustrations by
EDUARDO GARCIA

STONE ARCH BOOKS
a capstone imprint

Jake Maddox books are published by Stone Arch Books
A Capstone Imprint
1710 Roe Crest Drive
North Mankato, Minnesota 56003
www.capstonepub.com

Library of Congress Cataloging-in-Publication Data

Maddox, Jake.
Cycling champion / by Jake Maddox ; text by Martin Powell ; illustrated by Eduardo Garcia.
p. cm. -- (Jake Maddox sports story)
Summary: Austin, eager to win sports trophies like his older brothers, joins a local cycling club and enters his name for a three mile race--will he learn in time that bicycle racing is as much about technique as speed?
ISBN 978-1-4342-3290-8 (library binding) -- ISBN 978-1-4342-3904-4 (pbk.)
1. Bicycle racing--Juvenile fiction. 2. Competition (Psychology)--Juvenile fiction. 3. Brothers--Juvenile fiction. 4. Friendship--Juvenile fiction. [1. Bicycle racing--Fiction. 2. Competition (Psychology)--Fiction. 3. Brothers--Fiction. 4. Friendship--Fiction.] I. Powell, Martin, 1959- II. Garcia, Eduardo, 1970 Aug. 31- ill. III. Title. IV. Series.

PZ7.M25643Cy 2012
813.6--dc23

2011032459

Graphic Designer: Russell Griesmer
Production Specialist: Michelle Biedscheid

Printed in the United States of America in Stevens Point, Wisconsin.
092014
008484R

TABLE OF CONTENTS

CHAPTER 1
THE SUPER BROTHERS

"That's it. Nobody move," Austin's mother said. "Perfect! Now smile!" She was busy snapping another photo of Austin's twin brothers, Josh and Matt. The boys stood next to each other in the living room, proudly holding their basketball trophy between them.

It was easy for the boys to smile. Josh and Matt were great athletes, and tonight their team had won again.

Austin sighed. It wasn't the first time his older brothers had brought home a trophy. It wasn't even the second or third time. They won all the time. Austin was proud of his brothers, but he couldn't help feeling a little jealous. He'd never won a trophy for any sport.

"I thought for sure we'd run out of time before you made that last shot," Josh admitted to Matt.

"All I was thinking about was sinking that basket," Matt said. "I never even thought about the clock."

"Well, you were the only one," their dad said. "The rest of us were holding our breath!"

Austin knew he should congratulate his brothers. "Really great game, guys," he said.

"Okay, everyone to the table for pizza," Mom said. "Time to celebrate!" She turned and walked through the kitchen door.

Austin's dad and brothers walked out of the room, still talking about the game. Austin stayed in the living room. He looked up at the awards and trophies on the bookcase. None of them belonged to him. Matt and Josh had won them all.

I'll never win a trophy like that, Austin thought. His brothers played almost every sport there was: football, baseball, basketball, hockey. Austin didn't play any of those. It wasn't that he wasn't athletic. He loved biking. He was even pretty fast, but nobody won trophies for that.

Austin sighed. He didn't feel much like celebrating. He walked quietly out of the living room and upstairs to his bedroom.

I'll never be as good as they are, he thought, flopping down on his bed.

Just then, there was a gentle knock on the door. The door opened, and his mom poked her head in.

"Are you okay, Austin?" she asked. She came in and sat down next to him. "Don't you want pizza? You'd better hurry up before your brothers eat it all."

"I'm not hungry, I guess," Austin said.

His mother pretended to look shocked. She reached over and felt his forehead. "You don't have a fever," she said with a smile. "But I've never known you to pass up pizza before. What's the matter?"

Austin shrugged. "There's no reason for me to celebrate," he said. "I didn't win the trophy. Matt and Josh did."

Austin's mom patted his shoulder and nodded. "So, that's it, huh?" she asked. "Your dad and I are very proud of all of you boys. You know that, right?"

"But I've never won anything," Austin said.

"Winning isn't the only thing that's important," his mom said. "Aren't you the kid who started his own lawn-cutting business this summer?"

"Yeah. So?" Austin said. He shrugged. He didn't get what his mom was trying to say. What did cutting lawns have to do with winning a trophy?

"So," his mom explained, "it shows what a hard worker you are. You kept at it and never gave up. We're all proud of you for that."

"It wasn't that hard," Austin muttered. He knew his mom was just trying to make him feel better.

"Give yourself some credit," his mom said. "You know what? There's something I want to show you."

Mom stood up and walked out of the room. When she returned, she was carrying a newspaper. She lightly tossed it on Austin's lap.

"Check this out," she said. "The article about halfway down the page."

Austin was confused, but he picked up the paper. When he saw what his mom had been talking about, his eyes widened.

At the top of the article, the headline read: *Youth Tour de France-Style Cycling Race Planned.*

According to the article, a local cycling club would be hosting an event called the River City Criterium in one month. The criterium was a single-day road race held over a three-mile course of city streets. Several of the major roads in downtown River City would be closed off as part of the course.

Anyone between the ages of twelve and sixteen could enter. According to the article, all that was needed to enter was a bike and the $25 entry fee. The proceeds would go toward improving the cycling club's practice facility. The winner of the race would receive a trophy along with brand-new racing gear.

"Mom, this is awesome!" Austin said. "This could be my chance to finally win something!"

"I thought you'd be excited," his mom replied. "But remember that this isn't just about winning the trophy. It's not a competition between you and your brothers. Just focus on training for the race."

Then Austin realized something. "I don't have a road bike for racing," he said. "Just my mountain bike. I can't race on that."

"What about all that money you earned cutting lawns this summer?" his mom asked. "Tell you what. If you put part of that toward buying a bike, your dad and I will help with the rest. We'll even lend you the money for the entry fee."

"Really?" Austin said. "Thanks, Mom."

"Now let's go have some pizza," his mom said. She walked back to the doorway. "I told your brothers they had to save some for you, but I can't guarantee they listened."

"I'll be right there," Austin said. "I just want to look something up first." He moved over to his computer. He had bike research to do.

CHAPTER 2

THE NEW BIKE

Two days later, Austin nervously studied the street signs as his dad drove through downtown River City.

Austin had spent the past two days doing as much research as possible on road bikes. They were way more expensive that he'd realized. Most of the bikes had started at more than $1,000. Even though he had some money saved up, that was way more than he could afford, even with his parents' help.

Austin had almost been ready to give up when he finally managed to find a Regal Sport Road Race Bike on sale at a cycling store downtown.

I hope I got the directions right, Austin thought. Suddenly, he spotted his destination at the next corner.

"Stop, Dad!" Austin hollered from the passenger seat. "This is the place!"

His father put on his turn signal and pulled into the store's parking lot. He squeezed the SUV into a tight parking space and looked through the front windshield.

"Are you sure this is the right shop?" his dad asked. "It looks closed to me."

Austin opened his door and hopped out of the SUV. He stood on the sidewalk and peered at the store.

"I see a light inside," he said. "They're still open."

Austin hurried to the front door of the store. He heard a car door slam behind him as his dad got out and followed him up to the store.

The little bell on the door jingled as Austin pushed it open and stepped inside. He took a deep breath. The scent of the new paint, fresh oil, and rubber tires filled the air.

Austin glanced around the store. There were bicycles everywhere. They hung from the ceiling and were hooked on the walls. There were so many on the floor that it was hard to walk through the store. Austin made his way through the maze of bikes to the front counter.

“Hey, there,” a voice called. “How can I help you?” An old man stepped out from a curtained area behind the counter and smiled at them.

“Hi, I called this morning about the Raleigh road bike that’s on sale,” Austin said. “You were going to hold it for me.” He couldn’t wait to see the bike in person.

The old man’s eyes lit up with recognition. “You must be Austin!” he said, holding out his hand to shake Austin’s. “I’m Charlie Barker, the owner. I remember talking to you this morning. The bike is in the back room. I’ll go grab it and bring it right out to you.”

The shop owner disappeared back behind the curtained doorway. Austin could hear things being moved around in the back room.

At last the curtain swished open, and Mr. Barker wheeled the bike around the counter. It looked even better than it had online.

"Here it is," Mr. Barker said. "Good thing you called when you did. This is the last one we have in stock."

Austin studied the bike, from the front handlebars to the back tire. He reached out and ran his hand over the metal frame. He knew from his research that the frame was made of aluminum, which meant it was stiff, strong, and as lightweight as possible.

"The most important thing to look for in a racing bicycle is weight and stiffness," Mr. Barker was telling him. "That effects how well your pedal strokes move the wheels. It might not be the most comfortable bike you've ever owned, but it'll be the fastest."

Austin nodded as he continued to inspect the bike. The front and back wheels were closer together than on a regular bike.

"Why are wheels so close together?" he asked.

"That makes for quicker handling," the shopkeeper replied. "And see how the handlebars are positioned lower than the seat of the bike? That puts you in a more aerodynamic position when you're racing — you'll cut through the wind better."

Austin smiled. He could already imagine himself hunched low over the drop handlebars as he raced. *This is exactly what I need,* he thought.

"So, what do you think?" Mr. Barker asked.

"It's perfect," Austin replied. "I'll take it."

CHAPTER 3

A NEW FRIEND

"Are you sure you don't want a ride home?" Austin's dad called out through the open window of the SUV. "We could wrap your new bike in a blanket behind the front seats to keep it from getting scratched."

Austin shook his head. "No thanks!" he said. "I want to ride home and get a feel for the bike. I need to start practicing right away if I want to be ready for the race in a month."

"Okay," his dad said. "Be careful, and don't be late. Remember, your brothers have another basketball game tonight, and Mom and I expect you to be there."

Austin nodded, only half-listening. All of his attention was focused on his new racing bike. He couldn't wait to try it out.

Austin swung his right leg over the new bike and eased himself onto the seat. He gripped the handlebars and smiled. It was a perfect fit. Looking left and right for traffic, Austin put his feet on the pedals and took off down the street.

He headed for the bike path that ran from downtown River City to his neighborhood. The bike path was familiar. He'd ridden it a million times. But Austin couldn't wait to try it out with his new bike.

Hedges, trees, and storefronts flew by as Austin pedaled steadily, building speed. The wheels on the new bike turned smoothly. He shifted gears as he went around a tight corner and leaned into the curve. Austin hunched over the handlebars as he sped up coming out of the turn.

A yellow traffic light glowed up ahead. Austin slowed to a stop as the light changed to red. He could see the entrance to the bike path up ahead.

"Hey, cool bike," a voice called from behind him.

Austin glanced over his shoulder and saw Dylan Benson, a guy from his history class. He and Dylan had gone to school together since middle school, but they'd never really been close friends. In fact, Austin couldn't remember ever really talking to Dylan.

"I didn't know you had a racing bike," Dylan said as he walked closer. "Did you just get it?"

"Yeah!" Austin said. "I just bought it at the cycling store downtown. I usually just ride my mountain bike."

Dylan stood off to the side and admired the bike. "Man, I wish I could get a new racing bike," he said. "I have one, but mine's an older model. I'm actually having it tuned up at the cycling shop right now. I wanted to get it ready for the River City Criterium next month."

"Are you entering that?" Austin asked.

"Yeah, definitely," Dylan said. "All of the River City Racers are entering."

"Who are the River City Racers?" Austin asked.

"It's the cycling team I'm on," Dylan explained. "What about you? You're racing with your new bike, right?"

Great, Austin thought. *More people are planning to enter the race than I thought. That's not going to help my chances of finally winning a trophy.*

"Oh . . . I don't know," Austin said. "Maybe. I just got my bike, so I'm still getting used to it."

"Dude, you have to enter," Dylan said. "You can't let that bike go to waste. You should come to our practice tomorrow. We'll give you some tips."

"Practice?" Austin repeated.

"Yeah, the Racers practice every Saturday morning," Dylan said.

"Um, okay," Austin said. "I'll be there."

"Great!" Dylan told him. "We meet at the community center at eight o'clock to stretch and then head out from there. Make sure you come ready to ride."

CHAPTER 4
THE RIVER CITY RACERS

The next day, Austin woke up early to meet the cycling team at the community center. He was nervous to ride with the other racers. He loved biking, but he'd never trained with other real cyclists before.

What if I can't keep up? he worried.

Austin wheeled his bike out of the garage. He checked the air pressure in his tires and carefully oiled the chain like the shop owner had shown him the day before.

His brothers came out the front door just as Austin was finishing up in the driveway. Matt dribbled a basketball back and forth in front of him. Suddenly the ball bounced free and hit the front tire of Austin's new bike.

"Hey!" Austin said. "Watch it!" He leaned down and examined the spokes on the wheel, making sure there was no damage. The bike was fine, but Austin was still annoyed.

"Sorry," Matt said, jogging over to retrieve the ball. "We're on our way to the park to shoot some hoops. Want to come?"

"No thanks," Austin said. "I have to be someplace." That was true, but it wasn't the only reason. Playing sports with his brothers always reminded him that he wasn't as good as they were.

"Okay, see you later then," Josh said. He and Matt headed down the street laughing and bouncing the basketball back and forth.

Austin finished giving his bike one final inspection, checking the handlebars, seat, and pedals. Everything seemed to be in good shape. He pulled on his helmet, climbed on his bike, and set off to meet the cycling team.

The streets of his neighborhood passed by in a blur as Austin pumped his legs faster, picking up speed. Hunching over the handlebars of the racing bike felt very different from riding his mountain bike.

Mr. Barker was right, Austin thought. *This isn't very comfortable, but I'm definitely going faster.*

Austin shifted through all the bike's gears as he rode, making sure they all worked and changed smoothly. He was still learning and getting comfortable with the gears. It took some getting used to, but he was catching on.

Austin came to a steep hill and shifted into a lower gear to bike up the hill. Even at the lower gear, pedaling was more difficult. By the time he reached the top, Austin's legs were burning from the effort and he was breathing heavily.

Before he knew it, he was at the River City Community Center. A group of teenagers, all wearing colorful biking gear, were standing around outside when Austin rode up. An older man, who Austin assumed was the coach, stood in the middle of the group.

Dylan spotted Austin right away and waved him over. "Hey, you made it!" Dylan said. "I'm glad you came. Let me introduce you to Coach Brady and the rest of the team."

Dylan turned to the rest of the group. "Everybody, this is Austin," he said.

"Hey, everyone," Austin said nervously, waving at the group. Most of bikers smiled back. They seemed friendly.

"Austin just got a new racing bike, so I invited him to train with us," Dylan explained to the other cyclists. "He's racing in the River City Criterium too."

Just then the coach stepped to the front of the group. He clapped his hands to get everyone's attention. The group quickly quieted down.

"Okay, listen up, everybody," Coach Brady called. "The River City Criterium is less than a month away, so starting today we'll be focusing on training for that. A criterium is a race that includes a lot of pack riding and sprints, so we'll be working on building leg muscles, endurance exercises, and sprint training."

Coach Brady leaned over and picked up a stack of papers. He held them up for the group to see. "These are maps of the race route," he told them. "Everyone take one and pass it on. You should study this over the next few weeks. Get used to the course. In the meantime, let's get down to business."

CHAPTER 5

MASTERING THE MACHINE

"One of the most important things for all cyclists to remember is stretching," Coach Brady told the team. "Most of you already know that, but since we have a new rider with us today, let's go over a couple of the basics. Who can tell me why it's so important to stretch before and after you ride?"

Dylan raised his hand. "Go ahead, Dylan," Coach Brady said.

"Because cycling is so repetitive," Dylan said. "You have to stretch so you have flexibility and balance in the muscle groups you use over and over, like your hamstrings, hip flexors, and chest. If you don't stretch, those muscles tighten up, and then you can't ride as well."

"Very good," the coach said. "Let's go through some basic stretches before we get on our bikes."

Coach Brady walked the team through a standing quad stretch, a standing calf stretch, a hamstring stretch, and a hip flexor stretch. Then he had them do a couple of basic shoulder stretches.

"Why do we have to stretch our shoulders?" Austin whispered to Dylan. "Our legs are doing all the work."

"Yeah, but think about how much time cyclists spend hunched over the handlebars," Dylan whispered back. "You have to keep your chest and shoulder muscles loose."

Austin nodded. *That makes sense,* he thought. But he was starting to realize there was way more to cycling than just pedaling fast.

After they'd finished stretching, Austin and the cycling team spent the rest of the practice training. They did set after set of lifts, squats, and leg presses, all designed to build leg muscles.

Dylan explained that they needed to do plenty of aerobic exercises before the race. "You have to know you can at least ride for the full length of the race before you move on to the details," Dylan told Austin.

They also did sprint training. Coach Brady instructed them to ride as hard as they could for intervals of 30 to 90 seconds. Then they'd break for 90 seconds before sprinting again. By the time they finished, Austin was sweating and panting for breath.

When Austin finished practice that afternoon, his legs felt like rubber. He barely had enough energy to bike home. And they hadn't even biked the course yet.

His brothers were in the living room watching TV when Austin walked into the house.

"Whoa, what happened to you?" Josh asked, taking in Austin's sweaty clothes and flushed face.

"I had cycling practice," Austin said.

"I didn't know you were on a cycling team," Matt said. "Did they hose you down or something? You're drenched."

"We did a lot of sprint training on our bikes," Austin said. "There's a big cycling race coming up in a month that we're training for. I'm finally going to win to my own trophy."

His brothers exchanged a quick look. "You know it's not just about winning a trophy, right, Austin?" Josh asked.

"Easy for you to say," Austin said. "You guys have a million trophies."

"Don't get me wrong, winning is great," Matt said. "But we play basketball and football and everything else because we love to play. Not because we want a trophy."

"If you say so," Austin said. "I'm going to go get cleaned up for dinner."

I don't care what they say, he thought as he headed upstairs to shower. *I'm going to win the race and the trophy. And then I'm finally going to prove I'm as good as my brothers.*

CHAPTER 6
SMARTER, NOT FASTER

Over the next few weeks, Austin spent every free minute he had training with Dylan and the River City Racers. The River City Criterium was getting closer and closer.

"A good criterium racer needs experience," Coach Brady told the group at practice one morning. "Being fast and fit is only part of it. You need a good strategy, patience, pack positioning, and bike handling."

Coach Brady had them practice riding in a pack over the course. That would help the riders get used to the pushing and jostling that would take place during the race.

Riding with all the other cyclists so close together, especially around the corners, was scary at first. Austin knew that riding in a pack could be dangerous. Concentration was important to make sure none of the riders rode into each other. If one cyclist went down, the whole group could go down.

But Austin knew he had to get used to the tough conditions if he wanted to win. As Coach Brady had explained, a criterium meant riding close together and bumping throughout the race. Riders had to learn to hold their lines and go with the pack, keeping the distance between riders equal even through the turns.

When they weren't practicing with the River City Racers, Austin and Dylan rode together to build up strength and work on their speed. Racing in a criterium required speed right from the start. The race was only a few miles long. If a rider fell behind, there often wasn't enough time to catch up.

With all their training, Austin knew he was getting faster. Still, there was so much to remember. Focus on your breathing so you don't get winded too soon. Bend lower over the handlebars so you'll be more aerodynamic. Remember to glide with the pedals — don't pump them so hard. You'll tire your muscles out way more than you need to.

He and Dylan were doing some practice laps one afternoon when Austin realized he was actually in the lead.

He was about to congratulate himself. But then suddenly, he heard the hum of Dylan's tires on the pavement right behind him. Before Austin knew what was happening, Dylan shot past him on the inside, hugging the corner tightly.

When they reached the end of the course, Dylan was waiting for him. Austin slumped on the seat, his lungs burning.

"How did you do that?" Austin asked. "I thought I had you back there! I was pedaling as hard as I could!"

"But you didn't have to," Dylan explained. "It's not about being the strongest rider. It's about being the smartest."

"What do you mean?" Austin asked. "The fastest rider is going to win the race, no matter what."

"You have to be fast, but in a criterium, it's all about where and how you use your energy," Dylan told him. "Knowing when to coast will help save your energy so you can use it when you really need it. You need to save something to make your break and sprint at the finish."

Austin nodded. It was one more thing to remember, but it would help. With all this practice he was starting to feel like a real racer. He might have a shot at winning the trophy after all.

CHAPTER 7
LAST-MINUTE ADVICE

Austin woke up early the day of the River City Criterium. The morning dawned cool and clear. It was the perfect weather for a bike race.

Austin knew he was as ready as he could be for the race. When he thought back over the past month he'd spent training with Dylan and the rest of the cycling team, he couldn't believe how much he'd learned in such a short time.

Austin made sure to get down to the course early so he would have plenty of time to get registered. There was already a crowd gathered near the starting line when Austin arrived.

He signed in and moved off to the side to stretch. The criterium would get to full speed within the first lap, so he needed to be warmed up and ready to sprint right off the line. He'd have to get in position early.

Austin looked out over the roped-off course. He knew what he was in for. He felt used to the course after riding with the team.

Cyclists stood all around him checking over their bikes and making last-minute adjustments. Everyone was decked out in tight cycling gear and helmets. The riders all had numbers on their racing shirts.

Everyone seemed anxious for the race to start. Austin was busy checking and re-checking his racing bike from gears to tires. Everything had to be perfect.

Suddenly he felt someone nudge his shoulder. Austin turned around and saw his brothers standing there.

"Josh! Matt!" Austin exclaimed. "I thought you guys had basketball practice this morning!"

"We couldn't miss your first big race," Matt said with a smile.

"You've seen all our games," Josh added. "Besides, we've never been to a real cycling race before. This is really cool."

"Thanks, guys," Austin said. "I'm glad you'll be here to see me finally bring home a trophy."

Matt and Josh glanced at each other. "Remember what we told you before," Josh said. "It's great that you want to win, but have fun out there, too. That's more important than some trophy."

"But if I don't have a trophy, I won't be as good as you guys," Austin blurted out.

"It's not a competition," Matt said. "It's about doing something you like."

"Yeah," Josh agreed. "Go out there and do your best. If you win, great, but if not, at least you know you tried your hardest and had fun doing it."

"Good luck!" Matt said.

Austin was quiet as his brothers walked away. *Maybe they're right,* he thought. *Maybe the trophy doesn't matter as much as I thought.*

Across the crowd, Austin saw Dylan checking over his own bike. Even though they'd been training together for a month, Austin realized that Dylan had never said anything about needing to win the trophy. None of the River City Racers had. They all rode because it was fun.

A voice over the loudspeaker interrupted Austin's thoughts. "Attention, cyclists!" an announcer said. "The River City Criterium will be starting in five minutes. Please make your way to the starting line and get in position."

Austin walked his bike over to the starting line and got in position next to Dylan.

"Good luck out there," Dylan said. "See you at the finish line!"

"You too," Austin said. "I'll be the one holding the trophy!"

Both boys crouched low over their handlebars. Then, with the sharp crack of the starting gun, they were off!

CHAPTER 8
THE RIVER CITY CRITERIUM

Instantly, the street was swarming with cyclists battling to get to the front of the pack. Austin got off the line quickly and fought his way to the front. He didn't want to get stuck in the middle of the group, jostling for position.

The River City Criterium was a three-mile race. Each lap of the race equaled one mile. It was a straight shot for the first couple blocks, and all the cyclists pedaled furiously, trying to hold their positions.

Going into the first turn, riders fought for position on the inside corner. Taking the inside corner meant the route was shorter. But Austin remembered what Dylan had told him. *Don't try to be faster,* Austin thought. *Be smarter.*

Austin positioned his bike to the outside of the field of riders. It was easier to whip around the corners if you were on the outside of the pack. Riders on the inside of a turn had to brake more to make up for the riders on the outside coming closer around the turn.

As he went around the turn, Austin made sure to keep his inside pedal up and his weight firmly on the outside pedal. He knew his bike would lean to the inside going around the turn, and he didn't want the pedal to scrape the ground.

The pack of riders came out of the turn and headed into a straightaway. Austin straightened his bike and pedaled hard, powering the pedals with a smooth and easy motion. His leg muscles were nicely warmed up, and his breathing was strong and steady.

Austin tried to pace himself. He knew he couldn't exert too much energy too early. He had to save something for a sprint at the end. Out of the corner of his eye, Austin saw Dylan in the middle of the group, trying to fight his way free.

The second lap of the race flew by, and before Austin knew it they were heading into the third and final lap. Some of the riders were having trouble and starting to fall behind. Austin fought to stay near the front of the pack.

His leg muscles burned as he crouched down low over his handlebars and pedaled as hard as he could. He was grateful now for all the endurance training he'd been doing for the past few weeks. It was paying off.

Austin swung around the corner and headed into the final straightaway. He'd lost sight of Dylan in the tightly bunched group. The pack of riders was grouped so closely together that Austin could hear the others panting for breath. Everyone was pushing as hard as they could.

Austin dug down deep and gave it his all. He started to draw even with the leader. He could see the finish line looming up ahead.

I might actually win, Austin thought.

Out of the corner of his eye, Austin saw a blur of movement. Then, at the last minute, Dylan sprinted past him and flew across the finish line.

A second later, Austin crossed the finish line in third place. He slowed his bike to a stop and then moved off of the course, out of the way of other cyclists, to catch up with Dylan. On the sidelines, Dylan was surrounded by other cyclists from the River City Racers. Everyone was celebrating.

"Where did you come from on that straightaway?" Austin asked. "How did you do that?"

"It's all about practice," Dylan told him. "You can't expect to become an expert sprinter your first race out."

"Yeah, I guess," Austin said.

"You're not disappointed, are you?" Dylan asked. "You should be proud of yourself. A top-three finish in your first race is pretty impressive."

"No, I'm not disappointed," Austin said. It was true. "That was a blast! You have to show me how you came out of nowhere like that, though."

"I'll give you some tips at practice next week," Dylan promised. "You're still coming, right?"

"Definitely," Austin said with a smile. "You still have a lot to teach me. Besides, there will be more races. I'm just getting started."

ABOUT THE AUTHOR

Since 1986, Martin Powell has been a freelance writer. He has written hundreds of stories, many of which have been published by Disney, Marvel, Tekno comic, Moonstone Books, and others. In 1989, Powell received an Eisner Award nomination for his graphic novel *Scarlet in Gaslight*. This award is one of the highest comic book honors.

ABOUT THE ILLUSTRATOR

Eduardo Garcia has illustrated for magazines around the world, including ones in Italy, France, United States, and Mexico. Eduardo loves working for publishers like Marvel Comics, Stone Arch Books, Idea + Design Works, and BOOM! Studios. Eduardo has illustrated many great characters like Speed Racer, the Spiderman family, Kade, and others. Eduardo is married to his beloved wife, Nancy M. Parrazales. They have one son, the amazing Sebastian Inaki, and an astonishing dog named Tomas.

GLOSSARY

aerodynamic (air-oh-dy-NAM-ik)—designed to move through the air very easily and quickly

congratulate (kuhn-GRACH-ul-late)—to tell someone that you are pleased because he or she has done something well

gear (GIRH)—a set of wheels with teeth that fit together and change the movement of a machine

guarantee (ga-ruhn-TEE)—a promise that something will definitely happen

research (REE-surch)—to study and find out about a subject, usually by reading a lot of books about it or by doing experiments

route (ROOT)—the road or course that you follow to get from one place to another

suspended (suh-SPEN-did)—hung by attachment to something above

trophy (TROH-fee)—a prize, such as a silver cup or plaque, given to a winning athlete or team

DISCUSSION QUESTIONS

1. Imagine that you're getting ready to race in a criterium. What do you think would be the most difficult part of the race? Talk about it.
2. Austin used the money he'd saved from working to buy his new racing bike. Talk about a time you had to work to save up for something important that you wanted.
3. Training for the River City Criterium helped Austin make a new friend. Talk about a time trying a new activity helped you meet someone new.

WRITING PROMPTS

1. Because his older brothers are so athletic, Austin feels like he's never as good as them. Do you have any siblings? Write about your relationship with your brother or sister.

2. Even though he practiced hard, Austin didn't win the River City Criterium. Write about how you would have felt after the race if you were Austin. Would you have been disappointed? Happy? Upset?

3. Austin's brothers help him realize that there's more to playing a sport than just winning. Write about a time you learned a valuable lesson. What was the lesson and who helped you figure it out?

MORE ABOUT
THE TOUR DE FRANCE

One of the most challenging and well-known races in the world of cycling is the Tour de France. Once a year, the Tour de France takes place over a period of three weeks and stretches across France and surrounding countries.

While the length of the Tour can change from year to year, the grueling race typically covers a course of more than 2,000 miles. The shortest Tour, which took place in 1904, covered a course of 1,500 miles, while the longest Tour, in 1926, covered a 3,570-mile course.

The race is physically demanding because the different stages cover both flat and mountainous terrain. The course changes from year to year, but the finish always takes place in the same place: in Paris, France on the Champs-Élysées.

The Tour de France, which began in 1903, attracts teams and cyclists from all around the world. The field for the race typically includes 20-22 teams made up of nine riders each. Teams and cyclists must be invited by the race organizer in order to compete.

The Tour de France is a stage race. That means that the race is broken up into day-long segments, called stages. Individual times at the end of each stage are averaged to determine the overall winner. At the end of each stage, one cyclist wears a yellow jersey, which indicates the fastest average time at the end of that particular day.

Lance Armstrong, one of the most famous American cyclists, has won the Tour de France more times than any other rider. Armstrong won the Tour de France seven times in seven years, topping the field from 1999-2005.

GO FOR THE GOLD

When Kyle is assigned the track-and-field events at his school's Olympic Fest, he panics. He doesn't know how to do any of them! Will practice make perfect, or will Kyle embarrass himself in front of everyone?

Austin is determined to win a loca cycling race and prove to everyon that he's as just good as his olde brothers. But before he can race Austin has to find a bike, train and learn the course. For Austin it feels like a race just to get to th starting line!

WITH JAKE MADDOX

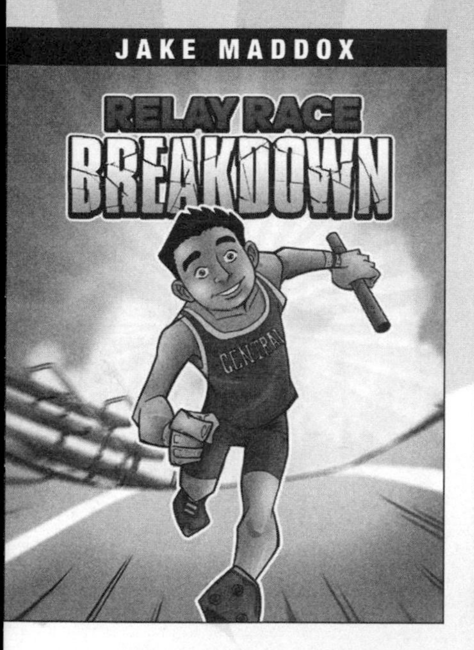

Nick hates running, but when his gym teacher gives him an ultimatum — join the relay-race team or fail the class — he knows he has no choice. He'll have to suck it up and run. Will Nick learn to run, or will he let down his team?

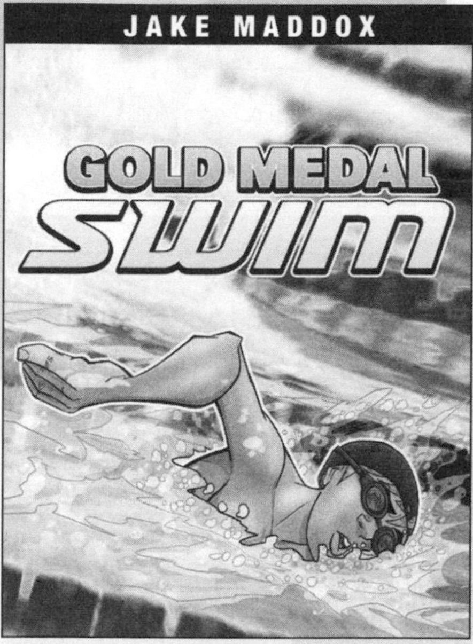

Sam is the best swimmer on his school swim team. When Julien, a new exchange student, joins the team, Sam offers to help him practice. But when Sam and Julien have to race against each other in the final meet, only one swimmer can take home the gold.